THIS BOOK BELONGS TO

For Clare and Rupert with our love

M. M. and E. C. C.

First U.S. edition 2011

Library of Congress Cataloging-in-Publication Data

Morpurgo, Michael.

The Pied Piper of Hamelin / [retold by] Michael Morpurgo ; illustrated by Emma Chichester Clark. — 1st U.S. ed.

p. cm.

Summary: The Pied Piper pipes a village free of rats, and when the villagers refuse to pay him for the service, he pipes away their children as well.

ISBN 978-0-7636-4824-4

1. Pied Piper of Hamelin (Legendary character) — Legends. [1. Pied Piper of Hamelin (Legendary character) — Legends.

2. Folklore — Germany — Hameln.] I. Chichester Clark, Emma, ill. II. Pied Piper of Hamelin. English. III. Title.

PZ8.1.M8265Pie 2011

398.2 — dc22 [E] 2010050683

11 12 13 14 15 16 SWT 10 9 8 7 6 5 4 3 2 1

Printed in Dongguan, Guangdong, China

This book was typeset in Historical FellType. The illustrations were done in pencil and acrylic.

Candlewick Press, 99 Dover Street, Somerville, Massachusetts 02144

visit us at www.candlewick.com

The PIED PIPER of HAMELIN

MICHAEL MORPURGO

ILLUSTRATED BY EMMA CHICHESTER CLARK

CANDLEWICK PRESS

I DON'T KNOW WHO MY MOTHER WAS, nor who my father was. There were a lot of children like that, like me, in Hamelin Town in those days. We lived in a shantytown of shacks around the garbage heaps outside the walls of the town, scavenging for scraps, like the crows, like the dogs, like the rats. Some of us were orphans, some simply abandoned. The truth is that most of us didn't know which, and it didn't much matter anyway. Either way, we were "thief dogs"— that's what the townspeople called us when they spat on us, threw stones at us, or set their dogs on us. And we *were* thieves too, there's no denying it.

But don't imagine there were just a few of us. The streets and alleyways of Hamelin Town were full of beggars and children like us. In every square, on every street corner, under every bridge, you'd see us. We had nowhere else to go. We begged because we had to, stole because we had to. When you're starving you have to, I promise you. There was no other way for us to survive.

Meanwhile, the rich and the greedy lived like kings and queens behind the walls and gates of their grand houses. And their children grew up — through no fault of their own, I've got to say — like spoiled little princes and princesses, with far too much of everything they wanted. Richest and greediest of all, though, was the mayor himself, and his councillors in the town hall. They were proud of it too, forever

showing off how rich and powerful they were, dressed in their ermine cloaks, with their shining gold chains and their sparkling jewels. And the mayor and his councillors were the nastiest of all the rich folk. The truth was that they were the real thieves. They'd gotten rich by taking money from the working people off the extortionate taxes they made them pay, more than three-quarters of everything they earned. But if ever they caught us stealing, they'd set their servants on us. They'd beat us with sticks and sometimes let their dogs loose on us as well.

To see me now, you'd think I'd been lame all my life. It wasn't like that. It was just bad luck. I was in the wrong place at the wrong time. It was a cold, frosty morning, I do remember that. So cold I could see my breath in the air. I'd been sitting on the corner of the Market Square, my usual pitch, playing my pennywhistle and hoping that some passerby would take pity on me and drop a coin or two in my hat. But my hat was still empty. I was tired, weak with hunger, and chilled to the bone after a night out in the open. I think that must have been why I fell asleep, and that was why I didn't hear the carriage coming, didn't hear the horses galloping over the cobbles. They were on me before I knew it. Somehow the horses didn't trample me. They told me afterward that none of them even touched me. It was the wheels of the carriage that did the damage. They ran right over my leg and crushed it. It was Emma who found me — she was my best friend and a thief dog like me. She patched me up as best she could. Emma saved my life, but there was nothing she could do about my leg.

Since then I've needed my crutch to get around. I can shuffle around on my bottom of course, but I'd rather not. It's very slow and it makes me sore. It's not very dignified either. Everyone said at the time that I was lucky to be alive. But to be honest, I didn't feel lucky. Anyway, I wasn't much use as a thief dog after that, only as a lookout. I couldn't thieve and make a run for it anymore like the others. I couldn't even climb the garbage heaps to go scavenging with the pack. Emma and the other thief dogs, they looked after me as best they could. I managed to survive. Just.

I could still play my pennywhistle. I could still beg. My leg — or perhaps my crutch, I should say — helped a bit too. Nowadays, a few of the townspeople seemed to take pity on me as they passed me by, and I'd get quite a few coins dropped in my hat, enough sometimes to buy myself a bread roll and even a bit of cheese too if I was really lucky. In spite of everything that had happened, I seemed to be doing all right.

But then came the rats — not just a few. No, this was a plague of rats. Like locusts, they ate everything in their path, and there were hundreds of them. Then before we knew it there were thousands, then tens of thousands, even hundreds of thousands. The mayor and his councillors did nothing about it, nothing whatsoever. It shouldn't have been a surprise to them, nor to any of us, not with the huge mountains of garbage piling up around the town. I mean, rats and garbage, they go together, don't they?

Of course we all knew that. We were used to rats. After all, we lived where they lived, in and around the garbage heaps. We ate what they did, and we ate them too — when we could catch them, that is. The trouble was that quite suddenly these rats weren't like normal rats anymore. They were massive: as big as cats some of them. Honestly. And they were everywhere, running all over us while we slept and eating up every scrap of food on the garbage heaps so that there was scarcely a thing left for us. Worse still, these giant rats were beginning to attack us. A cornered rat will always go for you, but these were hunting now, in packs. They had a dangerous look in their eyes, and we knew what it meant. We knew that they would kill us if they could.

Soon they had chased us out of our shacks, out of our shantytown, and off the garbage heaps altogether. We had nowhere else to run to but into Hamelin Town itself, where the rich folk lived and where we all knew we'd be very far from welcome. No one offered us food. No one offered us shelter from the winter cold. The rich children hurled abuse at us, threw stones at us whenever they saw us, and the mayor and his councillors set their dogs on us. At nighttime we hid and huddled where we could, under bridges, under carriages and carts.

Emma became such a true and faithful friend to me in those hard times. Now that the plague of rats was eating all the town's scraps, there was precious little left for us. Only the best scavengers were eating at all. To be a good scavenger, you had to be quick on your feet — and I wasn't. Emma helped me all she could, sharing whatever food she found with me. She stuck by me, looked after me. We broke into houses together, hid down in cellars or up in attics until we were discovered, as sooner or later we always were. Then people would drive us out with their cruel whips and their snarling dogs. The time came when there was no hiding place left and the two of us found ourselves with nowhere to shelter, almost always on the run. We were nearly starving and frozen half to death.

To begin with, while the rats swarmed over the garbage heaps on the other side of the river, the mayor and his councillors saw them as an opportunity for a bit of fun. They made great sport of it, sending out hunting parties on horseback, seeing how many rats their dogs could kill in a day, and which of them could kill the biggest one. They killed hundreds, and the more they killed, the happier they were. It was just a lark for them — but not for long. Once the rats began to come into town, to find their way into larders and into shops, the townspeople realized they could soon be staring starvation in the face. At last they began to take the situation more seriously. Now they went out hunting in deadly earnest.

For days the mayor and his councillors hunted down the rats and killed them. But then everything changed.

I remember the evening it happened. We were watching from the riverbank when we saw the mayor's hunting party come galloping back over the bridge into town. Then we saw the rats coming after them, swarming across the bridge in their thousands. The horses had their ears back. They were running for their lives, the dogs in among them baying in terror. I saw the look of panic and horror on the mayor's face as he came riding by us. All over town, as the rats poured through the streets, people were barricading themselves in their houses. In the Market

Square all the vegetable and fruit stalls, the cheese and sausage stalls, were stripped bare. In through the drains they came, in under the eaves, in through even the smallest of holes. In they came. It was an invasion, and within a few days it had become an occupation.

Everywhere you looked there were rats, in the streets, sitting watching you from window ledges, from the branches of trees. There wasn't a cat or dog to be seen in the streets. The rats were everywhere. These were angry rats. They'd bite you as soon as look at you. The mayor and his councillors tried all they knew to get rid of them. They put down traps, but the rats took one look at them and knew them for what they were.

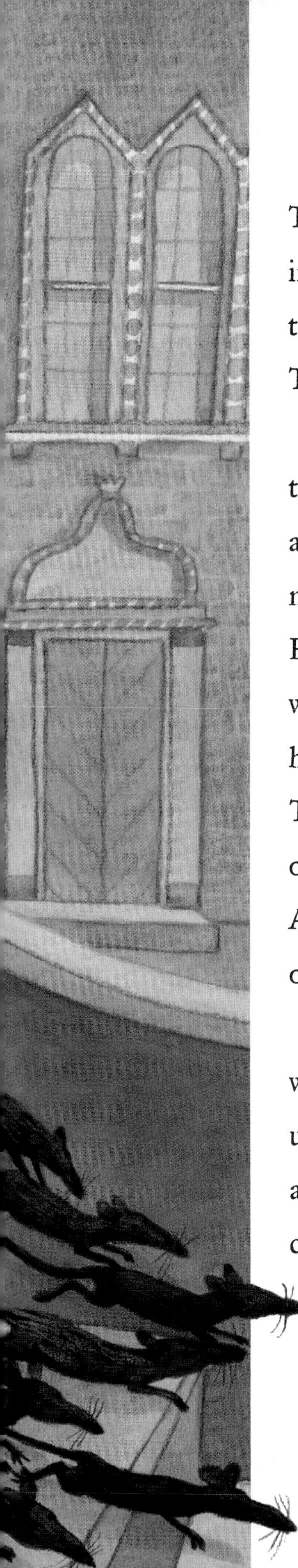

These rats were clever. They were super-rats! The mayor gave instructions to put rat poison down all over the town. But the rats took one sniff and realized at once what it was. It didn't fool them. They didn't touch it.

So the mayor sent his drummers out into the streets to try to frighten them away. This worked for a while, but as soon as the drummers stopped drumming, the rats came back. The mayor ordered that fires should be lit in all their nesting holes. He was sure this would drive them away. And it did too, for a little while, but as soon as the fires went out, the rats came back. It was hopeless. There seemed to be nothing he could do to rid Hamelin Town of the rats — nothing anyone could do. All they could think of was how to protect themselves and their children from the rats. As it turned out, it happened to be me that gave the mayor the idea of how this might be done.

One morning, I was standing on the steps of the town hall, with Emma beside me, playing my pennywhistle and begging as usual. We couldn't sit down anymore because the rats would try and bite us, there were that many of them. Even so, a couple of rats came right up to us, noses twitching, ready to give us a nip if we let them get any closer. They'd tried this before. But we knew what to do. I used my crutch and lashed out at them. Emma

always had a great long stick she kept by her for just this purpose. We were pretty practiced — had great aim too. The rats ran off at once, skittering down the gutter, squeaking and squealing as they went. That was when I heard a voice from behind us.

"They are frightened of you! You scared them off!" I looked up to see the mayor towering over me, all his councillors behind him. "From now on, thief dogs, you will be my rat boy and my rat girl. You will stay by me and my family twenty-four hours a day. You will keep these monster rats out of my house. You will drive off any rat that comes near us. You understand? For this I shall feed you — we have little to spare, but I shall see that you do not starve — and at night you may sleep in the town hall by the fire. Follow me."

It was too good to be true! We would have food. We would be warm. We would have shelter. So from that moment on we weren't thief dogs anymore. We became the mayor's "rat kids" instead, and we went everywhere he went, keeping the rats at bay — me with my trusty crutch, Emma with her great long stick. It wasn't long before all the councillors and all the rich people in town had rat kids of their own to keep the rats away from their houses. All the thief dogs had become rat kids. The rich people couldn't do without us. They fed us, they housed us — well, they had to, didn't they? But they still treated us like dirt, shouting at us and hitting us whenever they thought a rat came too close to them. But at least we weren't cold anymore, and we weren't starving, not for the moment anyway. That was something. That was a lot!

We rat kids did our best, but try as we might, we couldn't keep the rats from invading the rich folks' houses. There were just too many of them. Sooner or later they always got in somehow. They bit babies in their cradles, made nests in feather pillows, chewed their way into larders and corn bins. Day and night we kept after them, chasing them out and whacking them whenever we could. Day and night they came back. And of course we rat kids always got the blame, which meant that we'd get a good whipping.

Emma and me, we were luckier than most, not because the mayor was any kinder than the others — he most certainly wasn't. It was because I was a champion rat-whacker, an utter genius at keeping the rats out. The thing was, you see, I'd been using my crutch as a weapon for a very long time by now, so when I wanted to hit a rat, I didn't miss — ever. The rats weren't stupid — far from it. They knew what we were doing and they kept their distance, which meant they didn't bother us so much, nor the mayor and his family either. Because of this, the mayor was quite pleased with me and Emma, and kept us constantly by his side.

So that's how, on the day it all happened, Emma and I were right there and saw everything with our own eyes. We were there, at the council meeting, with all the councillors gathered around. We were on

the lookout, as we always were, for rats. The councillors were getting more and more agitated. Everyone was shouting over everyone else, complaining bitterly and noisily about the rats. What was the mayor going to do about them? Didn't he know that their children were being attacked in the streets on their way to school, that their wives were too frightened to venture out? Didn't he realize how serious the situation was, that there would soon be no food because the rats were eating everything, that butchers and bakers had closed their shops and fled the town, that the market had shut down, that Hamelin Town was facing starvation? What was the mayor going to do about the rats? The mayor had no answers. All he could do was sit there on his mayoral throne in a rage, blaming everyone, cursing everyone.

Suddenly, the great doors of the council chamber were thrown open, and in strode the oddest-looking man I'd seen in all my life. The whole chamber was at once struck dumb in amazement. None of us could take our eyes off him. This man was long and lanky, with a sharply pointed nose and darting, twinkling eyes that flickered around the chamber. He was so light and nimble on his feet that it seemed as if he were walking on air. And his clothes! You should have seen his clothes! He was dressed in a costume of brightly colored checks and patterns, with a hat on his head that had an enormous brim shading his eyes. He looked like some kind of court jester, or a traveling player maybe. All I knew was that whatever he was, he was wonderfully weird.

I noticed then that around his neck, on a fine gray cord, there hung a silver flute. He walked right up to the mayor and stood before him, his face bathed in the light from the window, his silver flute flashing like lightning in the sun. He glanced down at me then, noticed my pennywhistle, and smiled at me. A gentle, kindly smile it was, as from a fellow musician, one friend to another. But the smile was quickly gone, and he was suddenly serious again, his brow darkening as he turned his gaze on the councillors all around.

The mayor was on his feet by now, his voice loud with indignation. "How dare you come marching in here as if you own the place?" he roared. "Who do you think you are?"

"And good morning to you too, Mister Mayor," the stranger replied. He was very polite and soft-spoken. His voice barely rose above a whisper, but we heard every word. "I am known, wherever I go, as the Pied Piper. I am a righter of wrongs. It is what I do. That is why I am here. I heard that you have rather too many rats in Hamelin Town, and that you would very much like to be rid of them as soon as possible. From what I saw as I came through the town this morning, you do have a problem, a big problem. There are rats everywhere. I have come here to offer you my services, Mister Mayor. I can get rid of your rats, if you would like me to."

"And how precisely do you plan to do that?" scoffed the mayor.

"That is my business," replied the Pied Piper, calmly, quietly. "Believe me, if I say I can do something, then I can. I am a man of my word. Be sure you remember that, Mister Mayor."

"You silly-looking man. What makes you think you can get rid of the rats, when nothing and no one else has? I suppose, looking as ridiculous and outlandish as you do, that you expect them just to roll over and die laughing. Is that it?" The mayor was so pleased with his own joke that he began to roar with laughter at the Pied Piper, and all his councillors joined in.

For some moments the Pied Piper said nothing. He waited until the town hall was silent before he spoke again. "I came to rid your town of rats, which I can do very easily. I came to help you, and all you do is mock me. Is that any way to treat a stranger? I will not stay where I am not welcome. If you want to go on living with the rats, if you want them to overrun the town and drive you out, that's up to you. Good day." And with that he turned on his heel and began to walk away.

"All right, all right," cried the mayor. He was clearly having second thoughts by now; after all, this man could be Hamelin's only chance, its last chance, of getting rid of the rats. "Don't be so hasty. Just tell us how you will do it."

"I have my ways," the Pied Piper told him. "When I have finished, and I will finish inside an hour, the rats will be gone. That is all you need to know. But once the rats are gone, I will need some small payment for doing it, of course. By the look of you, I think you can afford it."

"You want money?" said the mayor. "No problem. We have plenty of money. Here's the deal. If you can rid us of these cursed rats, of every last one of them, I will give you all the gold coins you can carry. How's that? Would that be enough?"

"No," replied the Pied Piper, "it would not be enough. It would be far too much. One gold coin is all the payment I ask. No more, no less."

"I offer you a fortune, and you say one gold coin is enough!" The mayor simply couldn't believe it. "What's the matter with you? Surely you want more than that."

"No, Mister Mayor," replied the Pied Piper. "I am not a greedy man. Enough is always as good as a feast. When one man becomes rich, ten others become poor. Looking around this town, I think you should know that by now. One gold coin is my price. Let's shake on it, shall we? Then I know for sure that I have your word on it."

I saw the look on the mayor's face. He could not believe his luck. "Very well then, stranger," he told the Pied Piper. "I shall pay you one gold coin. It's a deal. It's a promise."

"I shall be back in a little while then," the Pied Piper said, "when the job is done. Good day, Mister Mayor."

Then quite suddenly I found he was speaking to me! "That's a nice-looking whistle you've got," he said. "Can you play it?" I couldn't speak. All I could do was nod. And with a smile, he turned away and strode out of the council chamber. I followed him as closely as I could. We all did. No one wanted to miss this. We were almost trampled in the crush as we made our way down the steps and out into the square.

We found the Pied Piper standing there. A huge crowd had gathered around him and was waiting in breathless expectation, wondering what was going to happen. Even the rats were no longer skittering about the streets, squeaking and squealing. They couldn't take their eyes off this strangest of strangers as slowly, slowly, he lifted his silver flute to his lips and began to play.

Music was never sweeter, never more serene. It was soft, as soft as the Pied Piper's voice, and yet somehow it filled the streets of Hamelin Town, floating its way into every alleyway, every garden. Whoever heard this music had to stop what they were doing. No one spoke. Everyone simply listened, entranced and amazed at the beauty of his music.

As for me, I was longing to get a closer look at the Pied Piper. I wanted to see how he played his flute, to discover how he could possibly produce such a rich and glorious sound. I mean, his flute may have been silver, but so far as I could see it wasn't much bigger than my pennywhistle. How was he doing it?

That was when I felt my whole body stiffen. I found myself frozen where I stood, unable to move a muscle. I could see that everyone else around me was the same. Nothing and no one moved in Hamelin

Town — except the rats and the Pied Piper himself. Then, as he was piping, he began to dance. Dancing and piping, he made his way out of the Market Square and into the narrow streets of the town. I saw then that the rats were following him, only one or two at first, then in dozens, and then in hundreds and thousands. Out of every nook and cranny they came, out of every house and home, down from the attics and the walls and the trees, up from the cellars and the sewers. Soon the streets had turned into rivers of rats, all running helter-skelter after the Pied Piper. In their mad rush to follow him, they skittered over our feet, clambering over one another, biting and clawing one another — anything, it seemed, to get nearer to the Pied Piper and his music.

Ahead of them, in the distance, I could see the Pied Piper still dancing, still piping, as he made his way down the street toward the river Weser, to where it ran at its deepest and widest and fastest. When he got to the bank, he stepped into a boat and drifted out into the river, playing his flute all the while. The rats followed where the music led. In their thousands, they rushed headlong, pouring down over the riverbank and plunging into the water — old rats, young rats, mother rats, father rats — until every last one of them drowned. Then, and only then, did the Pied Piper lower his flute, and the music stopped.

It was all over so fast. Suddenly my body came to life again. I could move, and so could everyone else. The whole town woke up around me. There wasn't a rat to be seen anywhere, not a single one.

As the Pied Piper came back up through the town, we lined the streets, cheering and laughing and waving. We flung our hats into the air, rose petals fluttered down from the windows, church bells rang out over the rooftops. The whole of Hamelin Town rejoiced. The Pied Piper soon found himself hoisted up on the shoulders of the townspeople and borne in triumph into the Market Square, where the mayor and his councillors were waiting for him on the steps of the town hall.

"Well, stranger, how on earth did you manage to do that?" the mayor asked him once all the cheering had died down. "Was there some

kind of magic in that music? What are you, a magician? Does that flute of yours cast some kind of spell? Hand it over!" he demanded. "Let me see it."

"I shall keep my flute, if you don't mind, Mister Mayor," the Pied Piper replied. "And please no more questions. That wasn't part of the deal, was it? All you need to know is that the rats are gone, every last one of them. I should tell you though, Mister Mayor, that they will be back soon enough unless you clean up this town — unless you get rid of those mountains of garbage. You should know that there's nothing rats like more than garbage heaps."

At this the mayor flushed an angry red. "Are you trying to tell me how to run my town?" he roared.

"I was only trying to warn you, Mister Mayor," said the Pied Piper. "I have been in many towns, in many countries, and this is the dirtiest by far. Dirt is why the rats came in the first place. Get rid of it and you will have no more trouble with rats. It's quite obvious really." The mayor, by this time, was spluttering with rage. But the Pied Piper simply ignored him and went on: "I haven't come back to argue with you, Mister Mayor. I've come to collect the money you owe me. One gold coin was the price we agreed to, I believe." And the Pied Piper held out his hand.

The mayor looked up at him, his face twisted with scorn and fury. "How dare you speak to me like that?" he spluttered. "Did you really imagine that I would pay you anything? You're no more than a wretched rat-catcher in a fancy suit who can whistle a good tune. You are a nobody — a nobody, you hear me? You can whistle for your money, rat-catcher, for I will pay you not a penny. What can you do? Can you bring the rats back? I don't think so. What's done is done, and you cannot undo it. Now off with you!"

The Pied Piper stood there looking hard at the mayor. He said nothing. The whole town was wondering what would happen next. I think we all knew this couldn't be the end of it; the Pied Piper wasn't going to leave it there. I was right beside him when at long last he spoke up. "Mister Mayor, I need to be very sure of this. Do I understand that you do not intend to keep your side of the bargain we made, that you are breaking your promise and will not pay the money you owe me? Is that correct?"

"That's right, rat-catcher," the mayor replied haughtily. "But here's a promise I will keep. If you are not out of my sight by the time I walk back to the town hall doors, I promise I shall set my dogs on you." With that he turned and began to climb back up the steps, the councillors following at his heels.

"I shall give you this last chance to pay me my gold coin, Mister Mayor," the Pied Piper declared. "If you do not, I promise you I will bring more grief to this town than you can possibly imagine. And believe me, unlike you, I am a man who always keeps his promises."

The mayor rounded on him. "You will give *me,* the mayor of Hamelin Town, a chance? You dare to threaten to me? You miserable rat-catcher! I'll show you who rules in this town." He turned to his guards. "Unleash the dogs!" he cried. "Let them tear him to pieces!"

At that very moment the Pied Piper put his flute to his lips again and began to play. The dogs,

already bounding down the steps toward him, were at once frozen in midstride. And now I saw that the mayor and his councillors, and all the townspeople too, had suddenly turned rigid where they stood. They couldn't move! It was just as it had been before, except for one thing. I could still move. I could move my fingers, my hands, my arms. I expected to find myself paralyzed like the others by the Pied Piper's magical music, but I wasn't. When I looked around me, I saw that all the children, poor and rich alike, from tiny tots to teenagers, were all beginning to follow the Pied Piper, dancing and skipping along, and I found myself hobbling along after them.

The music seemed to seep into my body, and I simply had to follow. I couldn't stop myself. I didn't even want to try. I wanted to go where the music took me, where the Pied Piper led me. I found Emma walking beside me. "Isn't it wonderful?" she said. And it truly was. It was as if he was leading us all by the hand, every one of us, and we knew that wherever we were going, wherever he was taking us, would be beautiful — as beautiful as his music. As we followed the Pied Piper out of Market Square, I looked back and saw the mayor and the councillors, all the mothers and fathers, grandmothers and grandfathers, standing there helpless as statues, quite unable to move. They could only look on in horror as all their children, every single child in Hamelin Town, followed the Pied Piper down the street toward the river.

I knew I wasn't going to be able to keep up with the others. Emma kept coming back for me to see if I needed help, but I told her I was doing fine, that I'd just follow the music, keep going, and catch up with her later — I never liked anyone fussing over me, not even her. By the time I got to the bridge though, they had already reached the far side. The Pied Piper was a long, long way ahead of me now, leading the way up into the hills beyond, the cavalcade of children skipping and dancing after him. And they were singing too. How I longed to be able to catch up, to be with them all! As hard as I tried, I couldn't make my one good leg and my crutch go any faster. But the music drew me, and I kept going steadily on. Where the Pied Piper went, I followed.

I hobbled past the garbage heaps, over the bridge and through the shantytown where I had grown up, ever onward, ever upward, along the rushing river, through farmland and forests. The Pied Piper and the children were so far ahead of me now that I could only catch occasional glimpses of them. But somehow I could still hear the sound of his flute as loud as ever in my ears, and I knew that all I had to do was to follow it. Sooner or later it would bring me to where the rest of them had gone, and everything would be all right. Time and again Emma came back for me, and time and again I told her not to fuss, that I could manage on my own, and sent her back to join the others.

For that whole day, all that night, and into the next dawn, I stumbled on without stopping once. How many miles I do not know. The valleys and hills, even the clouds above, seemed to ring with the Pied Piper's music. So weary that I thought my heart would burst, I came out of the forest into a broad green valley, looked up, and saw snowcapped mountains ahead of me, mountains so high and mighty that they touched the clouds. I knew at once that I couldn't possibly make it over those mountains. But the Pied Piper played on, and exhausted as I was, somehow I followed where the music took me.

It had been some time since I had seen even a glimpse of the children, but when I did at last catch sight of them, they were not as far away as I had expected. They were following a sheep track that wound around the mountainside. The Pied Piper was leading the way, and all of them were dancing and singing. Then, as I watched, the strangest thing began to happen. I could not believe my eyes! The mountainside itself seemed to be opening, just a crack at first, but then, with a great grinding and groaning, the crack became wider and wider, until there was a gaping black cave in the rock face. As I looked on, astonished and aghast, the children vanished into the mountain until only the Pied Piper was left.

"I'm coming!" I cried out. "Wait for me. Please wait for me. Don't leave me behind!" I waved at him frantically, calling out at the top of my voice. He must have heard me or seen me, because he waved back, beckoning me toward him. I staggered on as fast as I could go, but the track was tortuous and steep, my feet horribly sore, and my whole body heavy with tiredness. It took me a long while to catch up. I came around the last bend in the sheep track to see the Pied Piper disappear inside and the mountainside close again before my eyes. By the time I reached the place where the cave had been, there wasn't even the faintest trace of a crack to be seen. There was a young spruce tree growing out of a rocky ledge, a single edelweiss beside it. And there hanging on a branch was the Pied Piper's silver flute glinting in the early morning sun.

I put my mouth against the rock face and shouted for all I was worth. "Open up! Open up! Let me in!" But there was no answer. I was crying my heart out by this time. Again and again I called, but no one replied. I didn't know what to do. But then it came to me that there might be one last chance. I reached up, took his flute off the tree, put it to my lips, and blew, hoping against hope that the magic in the music would open up the mountainside again. No matter how hard I tried, I couldn't make a sound come out of his flute, not a single note.

That was when I first heard the sound of children singing, from deep inside the mountain, and then the voice of the Pied Piper himself. "Listen carefully," he said to me, his voice sounding far away and close at the same time. "Don't feel sad. I've chosen you specially as my messenger. I need to have someone who can play my flute when the time is right."

"What time? What do you mean?" I asked him.

"My flute is silent now, and it will remain silent until the mayor and his councillors have made the town well again, have made it a proper place to live. Go back to Hamelin and tell the mayor and all the people, from me, that if they want their children back, then they must make their town a fit place for children to live. Children should not have to grow up in a place where there is no honesty, where promises can be broken so easily, and where greed and wastefulness rule. There must be no more beggars, no more poor, ragged children living on the scraps from the rich man's table. There is enough to go around in Hamelin Town for everyone, and enough is all you need. Every child should have a clean place to live, food on the table, and a warm fire in the winter."

"What, everyone? Even thief dogs?" I said.

"Everyone," came the answer. "Instead of garbage heaps, I want to see parks where all the children can play, and schools where all the children can learn. I want to see fairness and kindness. I want to see the happiness that only fairness and kindness can bring. Only when I know that Hamelin is a fit place for children to grow up, can the children go home again."

"But what will you do with them? Where will they go?" I asked.

"Don't worry yourself. I shall look after them as if they were my own, I promise you," the Pied Piper told me. "I'm taking them to a place where they will all be happy. Tell them that in Hamelin Town. And tell them that they have a year and a day, that all I have said must be achieved by then. In a year and a day from now they must send you back here to the mountainside, and you must be alone when you come. When you return all you have to do is play on my magic flute. If everything is as it should be in Hamelin Town, then you will hear its music. If not, it will be silent as it is now, and remain silent forever. I shall be listening, and if I hear the music, the mountain will open up for you, and Hamelin's children will come home, and all shall be well again. I promise you. Take the flute with you now, and go."

"But what about Emma?" I cried. "What about my friends? I'll have no one to play with. I'll be all alone. Let me come in! Please let me go with them!"

I pleaded, I begged, but no answer came. He didn't speak to me again. Very soon the singing faded, and I was left alone and bereft on the mountainside. With a heavy heart I made my way back to Hamelin Town. All that day and the night that followed, I walked, until in the gray light of dawn I saw the town ahead of me. Even as I came over the bridge I could hear the weeping and wailing. The streets were completely deserted as I walked up into the Market Square. Every house I passed was a house of sadness, the doors and shutters closed. And not a single bird was singing.

I found the mayor sitting on the town hall steps, his councillors around him, sobbing and distraught with grief. It was the mayor who saw me first. He was up on his feet at once, his eyes filled with sudden hope. "Please tell me you are not alone," he cried. "Tell me the other children are coming back too. Is my son with you? My daughter?"

"I am on my own," I told him. "But your son and your daughter and all the other children are alive and well and happy. The Pied Piper told me so."

And then, as the townspeople gathered about me, anxious for news of their children, I gave them the Pied Piper's message. I held up his magic flute. I blew on it to show them that no sound would come out. I told them everything we had to do to bring the children home again. How in a year and a day, if we did all the Pied Piper had said, I would be able to go back up to the mountain. I would play the magic flute and the mountain would open up; the children would be released and come back home. I told them also, that if we did not change our ways, if by then fairness and kindness did not rule in Hamelin Town, the Pied Piper said we would never see the children again.

They listened in silence. By the time I had finished speaking, the mayor and his councillors could only hang their heads in shame.

Everyone in Hamelin Town knew in their hearts that they shared the blame and the shame as well. The mayor held up his hands and spoke to the crowd. "Good people of Hamelin, I ask your forgiveness. The Pied Piper is right, right about everything." And with that, he took off his ermine cloak and his golden chain of office, pulled the jeweled rings from his fingers, and dropped them all on the ground at his feet. "I shall give all I have," he went on, "do all I can from this day on, to make amends for the wrongs I have done. Will you join me in this great endeavor? We have a year and a day. Shall we make Hamelin a town we can truly be proud of — a place fit for our children? Shall we?" Everyone was cheering then, not cheering the mayor, but cheering the idea, the Pied Piper's idea.

We set to work at once, putting right the years of wrong. Over the next weeks and months everyone in Hamelin Town worked night and day to do all the Pied Piper had demanded of us and more. The shantytown and the garbage heaps disappeared first. Soon we had built enough proper houses for every family in town. We laid out the park, built a school. No beggars walked the streets anymore, and the sick and old were lovingly cared for. Everyone, the mayor and his councillors too, worked hard night and day to make this happen.

I went to my bed tired every night, but happy, because every night I dreamed of Emma and all the other children. I saw in my dreams how happy they were now, thief dogs and rich children quite indistinguishable from one another, playing and working together. I saw them herding goats in the mountains, harvesting berries and nuts, collecting firewood for the winter, paddling in the streams, running in the meadows, stomping in the mud, and climbing the trees. Sometimes, deep in my dreams, I would listen to the Pied Piper telling them stories at night around the fire, and I would see Emma laughing with the others, hear her laughing. I was happy for a while but I missed her. I missed all of them. I would tell my dreams to everyone in town. Like me, they all hoped and believed they were true. Everything I told them only made them long all the more to see their beloved children again. It made them work even harder to make Hamelin Town the best place in the world for children.

Through spring and summer we worked on, through autumn and winter, until the edelweiss flowered and the year came around again. With the old year behind us, and all the work done, the townspeople wanted to come with me up the mountain to fetch the children back. It was all I could do to make them stay behind. I told them again and again that the Pied Piper had said I must return to the mountain alone. But there was one question they kept asking me.

"You know the Pied Piper better than any of us. Now we have done all he asked of us, are you sure he will keep his promise, and let our children come home? Will he?"

"Of course he will," I told them. "If there's one thing we all know, it's that the Pied Piper takes promises seriously." But despite everything I said to reassure them, to calm their fears, when dawn came on that last day and it was time for me to leave, I saw anxious faces all around. They insisted I take the strongest donkey in town for the journey. I think maybe they were worried I might not make it in time, and of course, I was more than happy not to have to walk. So, riding on the donkey, with the Pied Piper's magic flute around my neck, I set out, watched from every window as I passed. I knew I carried with me the hopes and fears of every soul in Hamelin Town.

The donkey may have been strong, but he

needed some encouragement when he got tired. A gentle tap from my crutch from time to time was enough to keep him going. Up the hills and down the valleys he plodded on, along the rushing river, through farmland and forest, following the same track I'd walked the year before. We slept for a while under the stars that night, and in the early morning I found myself riding up the sheep track that wound around the mountain. At last I came again to the place where the young spruce tree grew out of a ledge of rock. Just as before, I found a single edelweiss flowering nearby. It was the right place.

I wasted no time. I got down from the donkey, took the magic flute with both hands, and with my heart full of hope, I blew gently. Nothing. Not a sound came out. I wondered then, for the first time, whether or not the Pied Piper had been telling me the truth. We had done all he'd asked of us, and still his magic flute was silent. My lips were dry, too dry. I licked my lips, took a deep breath, prayed, and tried again.

You cannot imagine the joy in my heart when I heard those first notes filling the air around me. It was the sweetest sound I ever heard in all my life, sweeter by far than any birdsong. It echoed through the mountains. I knew at that moment, and for certain now, that sooner or later, the mountainside would open up for me, just as the Pied Piper had promised. I didn't have to wait long. Sure enough, and with a great grinding and groaning, the rock face in front of me began to open up, and out they came. Emma was first, she threw herself into my arms. Then came the others, in ones and twos, in their dozens, in their hundreds, and last of all the Pied Piper himself.

He wanted to come all the way back with us, to see what the

townspeople had done, he said. So, with the Pied Piper walking along beside us, I rode back to Hamelin Town with Emma in front of me on the donkey. She loved donkeys, she told me. But I hoped it was more because she wanted to be close to me all the way back home. And as the children walked they danced and sang, while I played all the tunes I knew on the Pied Piper's magic flute. Even the donkey seemed to like it. His ears never stopped twitching and turning all the way home.

As we came at last into the town, everyone was cheering and crying and waving. Mothers and fathers, grandmothers and grandfathers, sought out their children and ran to them and caught them up in their arms.

On the steps of the town hall, the mayor and his councillors were waiting for us. They wore no ermine, no gold chains, no jewels. The whole town fell silent, all of us waiting to hear what the Pied Piper would say. I saw a sudden frown coming over him as he looked at the mayor.

"There is something you still seem to have forgotten, Mister Mayor," he said. The mayor looked very alarmed at this, and bewildered. "For getting rid of the rats," the Pied Piper went on. "You owe me one gold coin, remember?"

"But sir," replied the mayor, on his knees now, "please understand that we have spent all the money we had to make Hamelin a better place for our children to live, as you said we should. There is nothing left, not one gold coin."

The Pied Piper's face broke into the warmest of smiles. He put out his hand and helped the mayor to his feet. "That's all I wanted to hear, Mister Mayor," he said. "And now I must be on my way." He turned to go, and saw me standing there. "You play my flute wonderfully well, but I wonder if I might have it back now, if you don't mind." As I gave it to him, he smiled at me once more. "We did all right, you and me," he said.

Then, without another word, the Pied Piper walked away through the crowd, and putting his magic flute to his lips, he began to play. And we began to sing, the whole town together. We couldn't seem to help ourselves. We sang with such joy in our hearts, it was as if the whole world was singing with us.

THE END